P9-EMC-946

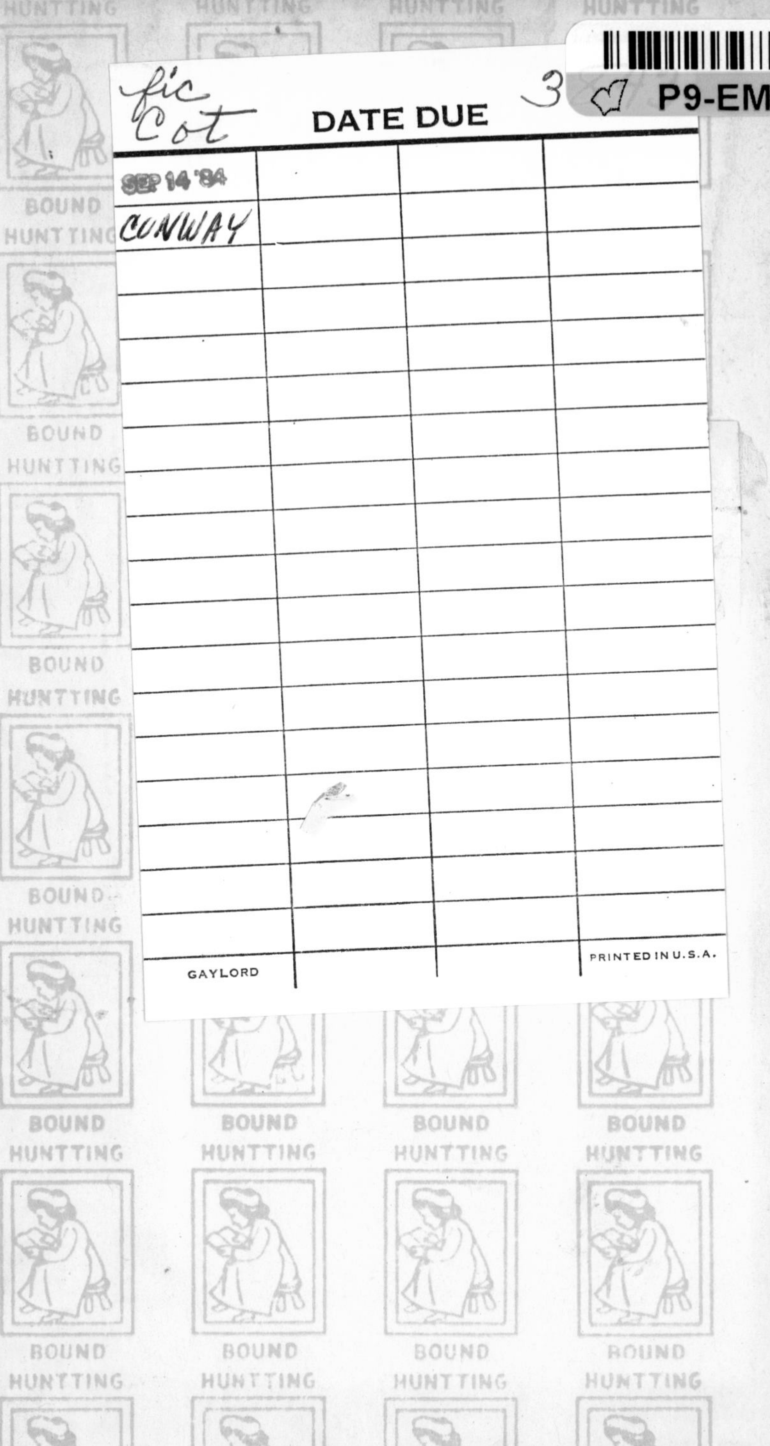
fic
Cot
3
DATE DUE
SEP 14 '84
CONWAY
GAYLORD
PRINTED IN U.S.A.

The Magic Calabash

Folk Tales from America's Islands and Alaska

Also by Jean Cothran

WITH A WIG, WITH A WAG
and Other American Folk Tales

The MAGIC CALABASH

Folk Tales from AMERICA'S ISLANDS and ALASKA

Edited by

JEAN COTHRAN

Illustrated by

CLIFFORD N. GEARY

DAVID McKAY COMPANY, INC.
New York

For France

Library of Congress Catalog Card No. 56-9093

VAN REES PRESS • NEW YORK

Acknowledgments

For permission to reprint, adapt, translate or retell the stories listed below, the editor is indebted to:

The American Folklore Society, for the following:

From the *Journal of American Folklore:*

"The Three-cornered Hat," translated and retold from #89, "El Sombrero Maravilloso" in Part I, *Cuentos Picarescos* in *Porto-Rican Folk-lore: Folk Tales* by J. Alden Mason, edited by Aurelio M. Espinosa, Vol. 35, 1922.

"The Horse of Seven Colors," translated and retold from #9, "El Caballo de Siete Colores," in Part III, *Cuentos de Encantamiendo*, in *Porto-Rican Folk-lore: Folk Tales* by J. Alden Mason, edited by Aurelio M. Espinosa, Vol. 38, 1925.

"The Fig Tree," translated and retold from #34, "La Vieja y Su Cabra," in Part IV, *Cuentos de Animales*, in *Porto-Rican Folk-lore: Folk Tales* by J. Alden Mason, edited by Aurelio M. Espinosa, Vol. 40, 1927.

From the *Memoirs of the American Folklore Society:*

"The Sailor and the Devil's Daughter," a retelling of #9, "The Devil's Daughter"; "Crafty Crab," a retelling of #13, "The Race"; and "Ol' Guinea Man," a retelling of #43, "He Calls the King's Wife a Liar," in *Folk-lore of the Antilles* by Elsie Clews Parsons, Part II, Vol. 26, 1936.

George T. Armitage and Mrs. Henry P. Judd for "The Magic Calabash," a retelling of "A Clever Hunter," from *Ghost Dog and Other Hawaiian Legends* by George T. Armitage and Henry P. Judd, Honolulu, Advertiser Publishing Co., 1944.

Professor Martha W. Beckwith for "The Wiliwili Trees," a retelling of "The Wiliwili Trees of Paula," from *Folk-Tales from Hawaii*, collected and translated by Laura S. Green, edited by Martha Warren Beckwith; copyright, 1926, by Martha Warren Beckwith.

Island Import Company for "Coral Sea Contest," a retelling of "The Whale and the Sandpiper," from *Legends of the South Seas*, Book I, by Eve Grey; copyright, 1954, by Island Import Company, Honolulu.

Smithsonian Institution for "The Cranberry Feast," a retelling of "The Man Who Entertained the Bears," from *Tlingit Myths and Texts*, recorded by John R. Swanton and printed in Bulletin #39 by the Bureau of American Ethnology.

U.S. Department of the Interior, Bureau of Indian Affairs, for "A Whale of a Tale," a retelling of "The Boy Who Ate Too Much," from *Igloo Tales* by Edward L. Keithahn, published by the U.S. Indian Service, 1950.

Contents

ALASKA

The Extraordinary Black Coat

THE SUN AND THE MOON LIGHTED THE FIRST DAYS, UP the Yukon. Then the sun and the moon disappeared, and for many months there were only the shining stars. The medicine men tried to bring back the two great lamps but their efforts were in vain. The darkness of night persisted.

Now in a village of the lower river, lived an orphan boy. His neighbors thought him foolish because he spent all his time listening to tales of magic. But he was just like any other boy—until he put on his extraordinary black coat. Then, in a moment, he became a raven, and a raven he stayed until he took off his coat.

After the shamans failed to bring back the sun and the moon, the orphan boy said to them, "What fine medicine men you are! Even I could bring back the light."

The angry shamans beat him for his insolence and

drove him from the meeting lodge. The boy ran to the house of his aunt.

"Tell me," he begged, "where the moon and the sun have gone. I wish to go after them."

His aunt denied that she knew their hiding place but the boy would not be put off. "I am sure you know where they are," he said. "Look what a finely sewn coat you wear. You could not see to make such little stitches if you did not know where the light is!"

Then his aunt looked him in the eye and answered, "If you wish to find the light, you must take your snowshoes and go south to the place you will know when you get there."

In the morning, black coat over his arm and snowshoes on his feet, the boy headed south. For many days he traveled, choosing his way in the darkness. Finally, far ahead he saw a gleam of light. As he hurried on, the light shone again, more plainly, disappeared, then shone again.

Presently at the foot of a hill, he came to a man shoveling snow from the front of his hut. Close by was the light, a great ball of fire. Every time the man tossed snow in the air, the light was hidden.

The boy began to wonder how he could make away with the great ball. After a while he walked up to the man and asked, "Why are you tossing snow so high that you hide the light from my village?"

"I am not hiding the light," replied the man. "I'm just shoveling snow from my door. What are you doing here?"

"It was so dark in our village that I did not like living there," said the boy, "so I came here to live with you."

"What! All the time?" asked the man.

"Perhaps," answered the boy.

"Very well, let me show you my home." The man dropped his shovel and, expecting the boy to follow, stooped low and entered the underground passage to his house. As he disappeared behind the door flap, the boy caught up the ball of light and started to run north.

Faster and faster he ran until his legs grew tired. So he put on his extraordinary black coat.

In the meantime the man had come out of his hut and called, "Boy, where are you?"

There was no reply in the gathering dusk.

"Boy!"

Then, although he knew the light was not his to keep, the man cried out, "Where is my ball of fire?"

The boy's fresh snow tracks answered him. The man hastened after them, only giving up the chase when the raven took flight. From the sky the boy saw him turn back, a tiny figure in a big white world.

From time to time as the boy flew on, he broke off a piece of the light and throwing it downward brought the day. For a while he soared in darkness, then he threw out another piece of light, making it day again. He continued to do this until he reached his own village where he threw away the last piece. Putting foot to earth, he took off his extraordinary black coat and walked to the meeting lodge.

Gathered round the fire, the medicine men were considering the light's return. Surprised by the boy's re-appearance, they stopped talking, and the boy spoke up.

"Now, you good-for-nothing shamans, *I* have brought back the light. Hereafter, it will be light and then dark so as to make first day and then night."

The words were scarcely out of his mouth before the shamans drove him from the lodge but they had to hold their tongues. For, as all the village could see, from that time on night followed day just as the boy had promised.

One morning after the boy was grown, he went walking on the off-shore ice. A great wind arose, drifting him on a floe across the water. Reaching the farther seacoast, he went to live in a large village. He took a wife from among its people and had three daughters and four sons. When he became very old, he called his children to him.

"The land of my fathers," he told them, "is across the water. It is my wish that you return there."

"As you will," they agreed, and his sons looked to their boats while his daughters made ready the household goods. Came fair weather and they left that coast for their father's country.

Up the Yukon they settled, living sometimes as people, sometimes as ravens. Their children's children forgot how to take off their extraordinary black coats, so ravens they have remained, even to this day.

The Cranberry Feast

TO THE RAVEN CLAN BELONGED AN OLD, OLD HUNTER who had outlived all his friends and family. He was so lonely that he often wished his days were at an end.

Early one morning, walking in the forest, the old man decided he would let the bears do away with him. He went to the mouth of a large salmon creek near his village and searched for a bear trail. When he found one, he lay down across the end of it.

Presently he heard the bushes breaking. A band of grizzly bears were coming his way. When the man saw how large was the leading bear and how white the tips of his hairs, he was overcome with fear. So when the leader approached him, he jumped up and, without knowing where the words came from, said:

"I am here to invite you to a feast."

The great bear's fur stood straight up. The man

thought his last moment had come, but he took a deep breath and repeated:

"I am here to invite you to a feast. I am lonely and would like your company at dinner."

At these words the leader turned and whined to the bears who were following him. Then, after bowing solemnly to the old man, he started to retrace his tracks. When the bears were out of sight, the man ran back to his village. Arriving home, he started to clean house. He put fresh sand around the fireplace, replenished the fuel pile, and looked to his supply of food.

The people in the village stopped to ask why he was making all these preparations. Since he had lost his family and friends, they had never known him to entertain anyone.

"I have asked some grizzlies to a feast," he answered.

His neighbors were amazed. "What made you do such a thing?" they asked. "They're our enemies."

He gave no answer.

Very early next morning the old hunter took off his shirt and painted himself with ceremonial stripes. He put marks of red across his upper arm muscles, a stripe over his heart, another across the upper part of his chest. With everything in order, he stood waiting outside his door.

When the village people saw the band of bears at the

creek, they were so terrified that they shut themselves in their houses, but the old man hastened to receive his guests. The same big bear was leading the band and when they arrived at the house, the old man took them inside and gave them seats. The bear chief he placed in the rear surrounded by the others.

The old man served them large trays of cranberries preserved in grease. First, the biggest bear seemed to speak to his companions. Then, as soon as he started

to eat, the rest started too. Whatever the biggest bear did, the others did also.

When the bears finished eating, the bear chief talked to the man for a long, long time. The old hunter did not understand the language but he gave his heart to listening. As the bear spoke, he paused every now and then to look up at the smoke hole as though deciding what to say next. After his talk, he left the house and the band followed him. At the door each licked a little paint from the host's arm and chest—a farewell salute.

The night after the feast the smallest bear returned in human form and spoke to the hunter. Whether he was awake at the time or dreaming, the old man himself could never say. The bear explained that he was a human being who had been captured and adopted by the grizzlies.

"Did you understand what the chief was saying yesterday?" he asked.

"No," answered the old man.

"He was telling you he has lost his friends and is lonely too. He wished you would think of him when you miss your companions."

So from that night, whenever the old man felt lonely, he gratefully remembered the visit of the solemn bear chief.

As for his neighbors, they were so astonished by the

bears' civility that, now, when they give a feast, they invite strangers—even if they are enemies. They seek to become friends with them, just as the lonely old man did when he once served cranberries to the great white-tipped grizzly chief.

Whistle the Winds

"GO OUT ON THE TUNDRA," SAID A WOMAN TO HER husband, "and bring me a piece of the tree that grows there."

"Only the wind's on the tundra," he answered. "No trees grow on that snowy waste."

"Go and see," urged the woman. "Perhaps you will find just one."

"What do you want with it?"

"I want you to carve me the image of a small boy. We have no children of our own and I am lonely."

As the man left his house by the Yukon river, there spread before him a path of bright light. Along this path he traveled until he saw, far ahead, a shining object. Going closer, he found it to be a little tree. He took his hunting knife, cut off a branch, and carried it home.

While the man carved an image of a small boy, his wife busied herself making a fur suit for the little figure.

"There's wood to spare," said the woman. "Make a set of toy dishes."

"What good will that do?" asked the man.

"It will give us something to play with."

So the man carved the tiny dishes and when the small figure was dressed, the woman placed him on the bench of honor opposite the doorway. Before him she put the dishes, full of food and water.

That night after the man and woman had gone to bed, they heard a low whistle.

The woman shook her husband saying, "Did you hear that whistle?"

"Yes," he answered.

"Do you think it was the little boy you carved?"

"No," said the man, but they got up, lighted a lamp and saw that the dishes of food and water were empty. The little figure was just where they had left him. His eyes, however, were blinking.

"Little Whistler," cried the woman in delight, "you're coming alive!" She picked him up and played with him far into the night. At last she put him back on the bench and went sleepily to bed.

In the morning when the man and woman woke, the small figure was gone. They searched for him all over the house before they saw his footprints in the snow outside the door. His tracks led them along the bank of a creek beyond the village. Suddenly the footmarks ended. Their whistling boy had taken to the same path of light which the man had followed when he found the shining tree. The man and woman could go no further. Slowly they turned homeward.

Along the bright path traveled the boy. At last he came to the edge of day where the sky comes down to earth and walls in the light. There in the east he saw a gut-skin cover fastened over a hole in the sky. It was bulging inward. He stopped and said, "It's very quiet here. I think a little wind will make it better."

He whistled while he drew his knife and cut loose the cover at the edge of the hole. Immediately, a strong wind blew in bringing with it every now and then a live reindeer.

The boy looked through the hole into another world. Then he replaced the cover and bade the wind not to blow too hard, saying,

> "Sometimes hard, sometimes light,
> Sometimes bless, sometimes bite,
> Blow, wind, blow!"

Leaving the east, he walked the sky wall until he came to an opening in the south. Whistling, he loosened the cover and in rushed a warm wind, laden with sea spray and rain. Before closing this hole, the boy said again,

> "Sometimes hard, sometimes light,
> Sometimes bless, sometimes bite,
> Blow, wind, blow!"

Then he passed to the west and as soon as the cover there was cut, in whipped the wind, needled with sleet. Once more the boy spoke,

> "Sometimes hard, sometimes light,
> Sometimes bless, sometimes bite,
> Blow, wind, blow!"

Along the sky wall to the north, the cold became so deep, the boy hesitated before whistling in a shrill blast which soon hid the earth with great snowdrifts. Quickly he closed the north hole and, having given his usual warning, traveled on until he came to the middle of the earth. There, lost in wonder, he looked at the tall lustrous poles which supported the arching sky.

One foot after another, the boy marched on until he found himself again in the Yukon river village. From house to house he went, making friends with the people and telling them to beware the wind. The last house in the village belonged to the couple who had made him from the shining tree. He whistled outside their door.

The woman raised the door flap.

"Little Whistler!" she cried joyfully and caught him up in her arms. "Look," she called to her husband, "our boy is back."

Welcomed by the man and his wife, the boy who whistled the winds stayed with them many winters. As he admonished it, so the wind has blown to this day.

Sometimes hard, sometimes light,
Sometimes bless, sometimes bite,
Blow, wind, blow!

Whale of a Tale

IN AN IGLOO BY THE SEA A BOY ONCE LIVED WITH AN old, old woman. This old, old woman was satisfied with little more to eat than the fresh salt air but the boy was always hungry. He never had enough. One day there was not a scrap of blubber left in the igloo and the old, old woman said, "Today, you can go to the shore and search for your own food."

So by the light of the midnight sun, the boy walked along the edge of the water and he had not gone far when he saw a tomcod. Leaning down, with one hand he grabbed its tail, with the other pulled off its head, and swallowed it in one gulp.

Walking farther up the beach, he came to a seal. As he had with the cod, he caught the seal with one hand, pulled off its head with the other, and gulped it down.

Smacking his lips, he walked on until he saw a large oogrook sunning itself on the sand. As he had the cod and the seal, the boy caught the oogrook with one hand, before it could escape into the water, pulled off its head, and gulped it down.

Being a little greedy, the boy went on up the beach

looking for something more. Caught on the high, dry sandbank lay a white whale. As he had with the cod and the seal and the oogrook, the boy caught the whale with one hand, pulled off its head with the other, and gulped it down bones, blubber, and all.

When the boy had eaten the whale, he felt so happy that he began to sing. First it was just a little hum, then the song grew louder and louder until it told all his wet and lonely world that for once he had had enough to eat.

After he stopped singing, he realized he was thirsty so he searched for a pond. Then he drank and drank and drank until the pond was dry. Turning around, he walked slowly back to the igloo where he lived with the old, old woman.

At the door he tried to go in. But he had eaten too much; he could not get through.

"How can I get in?" called the boy to the old, old woman.

"Come through the window," she said.

The window was smaller than the door, but he tried. His head went through. That was as far as he could go.

"Can't get through the window," he called to the old, old woman.

"Try the smoke hole," she answered.

"Ridiculous," thought the boy, for the smoke hole was smaller than the window, yet he gave it a try. This time his shoulders as well as his head went through but that was as far as he got, so he called:

"Can't get through the smoke hole."

"Come in through the eye of my needle," advised the old, old woman holding up her needle. Through it the boy tumbled onto the igloo's floor. The old, old woman saw how large he had grown from eating so much.

"Watch out!" she cried. "Stay away from the seal oil lamp!"

But the boy stumbled towards the flame as the lamp sprang towards him. Bang! There was a sound like a thunderclap.

When the crash was over the old, old woman found herself outside the igloo. She crept to the window and looked in. The boy had disappeared. The lamp was not to be seen. Where the floor had been was a deep, dark pool. In it swam slowly round and round a tomcod, a seal, an oogrook, and a big, white whale.

Dance, Raven, Dance

ONCE A RAVEN WAS FLYING OVER A REEF NEAR THE seashore. Some sea birds perched on the rocks caught sight of him and cried out, "Oh, you black one! Oh, you carrion eater! Oh, you black one!"

The raven turned and flew away screaming, "Gnak, gnak, gnak! Why do they pick on me?"

He skimmed across the great water until he came to a mountain on the other side, where he stopped. Looking about he saw just in front of him a marmot hole. The raven stood by the hole, watching. Very soon the marmot came back from a foray. When he saw the raven in front of his door, he asked him to stand aside. The raven refused saying, "They call me carrion eater, and I will show them that I am not, for I will eat you."

"All right," answered the marmot. "I have heard that you are a very fine dancer. If you will dance, I will sing and then you can eat me, but I wish to see you dance before I die."

The marmot's words pleased the raven so much that he agreed to dance. As the raven danced, the marmot sang, "Oh, Raven, Raven, Raven, dance, Raven, dance! Oh, Raven, Raven, Raven, how well you dance!"

Then they stopped to rest and the marmot said, "I am very pleased with your dancing. Now I will sing once more, so shut your eyes and dance your best."

The raven closed his eyes and hopped clumsily about while the marmot sang, "Oh, Raven, Raven, Raven, what a graceful dance! Oh, Raven, Raven, Raven, what a dunce you are!"

Then the marmot, with a quick run, darted between the raven's legs and was safe in his hole. From his doorway, the marmot put out the tip of his nose and laughed, "Chi-kik-kik, chi-kik-kik, chi-kik-kik. You are a clown! I could hardly keep from laughing. Now look at me. See how fat I am! Don't you wish you could eat me?"

And the credulous raven flew away in a rage.

HAWAII

The Magic Calabash

ON THE ISLAND OF HAWAII THERE ONCE LIVED A KING with the long and imposing name, Keawenui-a-umi. In the cool of an evening he liked to walk in his ohia grove, but these peaceful hours were spoilt by the raucous calling of birds perched high in the trees.

"Quiet!" commanded the king shaking his royal staff.

They answered with louder screeches.

"Silence!" the king ordered but the air filled with mocking chatter.

The king could not understand the birds' cries, but the tone of their voices was insulting. Somehow it reminded him that he was unpopular with his people, perhaps because of his over-bearing pride. At last he decided to rid himself of the noisy flock. But the birds always stayed out of easy aim, and besides he was not much of a marksman, so he asked the help of Mainele, a skilled hunter.

Possessed with the idea that the birds must go, the

king told Mainele, "If you kill these impertinent creatures, I promise you my daughter's hand in marriage."

"I will do my utmost to carry out your wishes," Mainele assured the king, for the princess had a kind heart as well as a merry twinkle in her eye.

Mainele's self-esteem was a match for the king's. There was no doubt in his mind that he could wing the birds and win a royal wife as he went deep into the forest to find wood for the straightest, surest arrows he could make.

Meanwhile, news of the king's unusual offer went as fast as the wind to the neighboring islands. On Kauai it reached the ears of Pikoi, an adventurous youth whose reputation with the bow was so great that rumor said he had once speared ten rats and a bat with a single arrow.

Pikoi decided he too would like to try downing the king's birds. Keeping his plans to himself, he quickly launched his outrigger canoe and set off for Hawaii. With him he carried his best bow and finest arrows. His strokes were fast and strong. He had heard how very charming was the princess.

On the island of Hawaii he beached his canoe and hastened to the edge of Keawenui-a-umi's ohia grove. A crowd had gathered to hear the outcome of the contest. Although Mainele had shot many arrows, he had failed to drop a single annoying bird.

In a rage, the king announced that the offer he made was open to any hunter who wished to try his luck. Immediately Pikoi made himself known.

"I am Pikoi from Kauai," he said. "I wish to accept the challenge."

"Very well," answered the king's servant and motioned him to come forward.

"Have you a large calabash full of clear spring water?" asked Pikoi.

"We will send for one," the servant told him.

While Pikoi waited for the calabash, the people wagged their tongues. Remembering that islanders long ago had turned many a trick with magic mirrors of water, they were eager to see if Pikoi could bring down the birds in the same way.

When the calabash was brought, the young archer followed the servant into the ohia grove where the king was pacing angrily between the trees. The birds screamed loudly overhead. Setting down the calabash in an open space, Pikoi quietly took a long look into it. The mirror-like surface of the water reflected the exact position of the birds perched in the treetops. Turning and aiming carefully, Pikoi let fly an arrow. With that shot he impaled every one of the birds!

The crowd cheered and the princess smiled at Pikoi. The magic of the calabash had won a royal bride for the marksman from Kauai.

The Queen's Riddles

LOOKING OVER HIS FIELDS AND FORESTS ON OAHU, A chief once boasted of their beauty to a stranger.

"I can see the lands of Wakea and Papa and they are larger and fairer than these fine places of yours," replied the far-sighted man.

"Fairer than mine?" exclaimed the chief. "I would like to see a land fairer than mine! Let's go there together."

They set out before dawn and soon came to a stranger standing by a coconut palm.

"What are you doing here?" asked the chief.

"I am Mama-loa, the Swift One. I am waiting for the sun to rise so that I may run and catch him."

"We will wait with you," said the chief.

"You must join us," added Ike-loa, the Far-Sighted, who could see the lands of Wakea and Papa.

When the sun came out of the ocean and started to

rise above the island, the Swift One ran very fast and caught him. He tied him up and held him prisoner for a time. Then the three traveled on together.

Presently they saw two men sleeping at the edge of the path. One was shivering with cold. His name was Kanaka-make-anu, the Man-Who-Dies-in-the-Cold. The other was burning as if he were on fire. His name was Kanaka-make-wela, the Man-Who-Dies-in-the-Fire. The travelers warmed one and cooled the other, and the five went on together.

In a rat-shooting field they found a man who displayed great skill with his bow and arrows. His name was Pana-pololei, the Straight-Shooter. They asked him to go with them to the lands of Wakea and Papa. He joined them and the six journeyed on together.

By and by beside a pandanus plant, they met a man with his ear to the ground.

"Why are you lying here?" asked the chief.

The man looked up and said, "I have been listening to the quarrel between Papa and Wakea."

"Come with us. We are going to their country," replied the chief to Hoo-lohe-loa, the Man-Who-Could-Hear-Afar-Off.

So the seven journeyed on until they came to Nuuanu Valley, the home of Papa and Wakea, ancestors of the

Hawaiian people. It was a more beautiful land than any of them had ever known.

Watchmen saw the seven fine-looking men and quickly sent word to their queen. Her warriors met the strangers and brought them to her house. There they were entertained and spent the night.

In the morning the visiting chief said to the queen, "I have heard that you set forth hard riddles. If I guess your riddles, will you become my wife?"

To this she agreed and lost no time in presenting the first riddle. "The man who is my brother is standing by the door of Wakea and Papa's house. Where is that door?"

The chief turned to the Far-Sighted One and whispered, "Can you see the door of Wakea and Papa's house?"

After looking all around, the Far-Sighted One answered, "The door is in the trunk of that great tree. If you are strong enough, break the bark and find it."

The chief went over to the great tree, tore away the bark, and opened the door.

Immediately, the queen spoke the second riddle. "There are three dogs. One belongs to Wakea, one to his wife, Papa, and one is mine. Point out the dog belonging to each of us."

The chief whispered to the Man-Who-Could-Hear-Afar-Off, "Listen and find out the colors of the dogs."

So Hoo-lohe-loa put his ear to the ground and heard Papa telling her servants, "My black dog must go out first; then Wakea's red one; and last, the queen's white hound."

Thanks to his friend, when the black dog leaped through the tree door, the chief cried out, "There goes

Papa's black dog." As the red dog followed, he said, "There is Wakea's." And, "That one is yours, O, queen," he added, when out jumped the white hound.

Amazed at how quickly her riddles had been solved, the queen soon put before the chief another proposal.

"The sweet water for our wedding feast has to be brought from a far spring," she said. "Send one of your men and I will send one of my women. If your man brings back his calabash first, you and I will marry at once."

The chief agreed and called the Swift One. He gave him a calabash and told him to take his place on the starting line.

In a twinkling the Swift One and the woman were off. The man ran smoothly, certain that there was no one in the world as fast as he, but the woman sped past him. The chief called the Straight-Shooter who sent an arrow flying close to the woman's head. Startled, she stumbled and the man passed on ahead of her.

After a while the chief asked the Far-Sighted One, "How are they running now?"

"The woman is winning again," he replied.

The chief turned to the Straight-Shooter. "Perhaps you have another arrow?"

A second time the Straight-Shooter's arrow almost grazed the woman. As she tripped, the Swift One rushed to the spring, filled his calabash and started back. But making a good recovery, the woman dipped her calabash, turned and sped by the man.

Straight-Shooter raised his bow and a third arrow shot forth. It whizzed by the woman causing her to fall. Her calabash broke, spilling all the water. The Swift One didn't pause until he had brought his brimming calabash to the chief who poured some water into a coconut cup and offered the queen a drink.

Meanwhile, the winner, instead of receiving the praise he expected, became the laughing stock of his five companions.

"So you think *you* won that race," they joked.

"Certainly," said the Swift One. "You saw me come back first. Why do you laugh?"

They laughed the more.

"*You* won it! Ho, ho, ho! Listen, Swift One, you and the Far-Sighted One and the Straight-Shooter together brought back that calabash." Then they told him how carefully he had been watched and aided by the well-timed arrows.

But the chief thanked all his friends for their help. He told them to listen carefully now for the queen was about to announce two more hurdles that had to be jumped before the wedding could take place.

"In this land," the queen said, "there are two spots,

one very hot and one very cold. Men must be found to live in them."

"Very well," replied the chief and called the Man-Who-Dies-in-the-Cold. "Perhaps you would go to the very hot place for the queen?" he asked.

Then he turned to the Man-Who-Dies-in-the-Fire and asked if he would go to the cold place.

"We will," answered the two, "but we'll never come back. Those are our natural dwelling places."

There were no more riddles to solve so the chief and the queen were married and together delighted in the beautiful land of Wakea and Papa.

Coral Sea Contest

SPOUTING AND DIVING, DIVING AND SPOUTING, A GREAT whale was playing off an island in the South Seas. He capered through the turquoise waters and then entered a lagoon where a little sandpiper waded in the reeds at the tide's edge.

With swagger the whale announced, "There are more whales than sandpipers in the world."

The sandpiper cocked his head, took a look at the leviathan, and went on running after crawfish. The whale circled out to sea before returning as near as he dared to the shore. Again he said, "There are more whales than sandpipers in the world."

His sudden reappearance caused the sandpiper to miss a tasty morsel. Annoyed, the bird replied, "Not at all. There are more sandpipers than whales."

"More whales," said the great fish.

"More sandpipers," answered the bird.

"I can prove it," said the whale.

"Go ahead," taunted the sandpiper.

Then the great whale in sonorous tones began to chant:

> "Brothers of the deep, O brothers of the deep!
> Ho! for the coral strand.
> Show yourselves near this land.
> Break your blue sleep, shake your blue sleep!"

To the east and the west chanted the whale. To the north and the south he chanted. From the east and the west came his brother whales, from the north and the south they gathered until, from the lagoon to the horizon, the water was alive with their glistening bodies.

"See!" said the whale to the sandpiper.

"You wait and see," answered the little sandpiper and he began to trill a song of his own:

> "Fair-feathers, fair-feathers,
> Sail the spiced breeze.
> Haste to these sandy-shored
> Bright southern seas."

The sandpiper sang to the east and the west. To the north and the south, he sang. From the east and the west came his brother sandpipers. From the north and the south they winged in, and the air was filled with the rustle of feathers as row after row of birds closed ranks.

"There," said the sandpiper.

"Where?" asked the whale, unimpressed. He dove out to sea and began to chant again:

"Brothers of the deep, O brothers of the deep!
Ho! for the coral strand.
Show yourselves near this land.
Break your blue sleep, shake your blue sleep!"

To the east and the west chanted the whale. To the north and the south he chanted. From the east and the west came his brothers, the sharks. From the north and the south they gathered, filling the far waters.

"Look," cried the whale, "there are many more whales than sandpipers."

"So?" questioned the sandpiper and began to trill again:

"Fair-feathers, fair-feathers,
Sail the spiced breeze.
Haste to these sandy-shored
Bright southern seas."

The sandpiper sang to the east and the west. To the north and the south he sang. From the east and the west came his brothers, the cranes. From the north and the south they wheeled in and, poised on one leg, waited to be counted.

"Look," called the sandpiper, "there are many more sandpipers than whales."

But the whale would not call it quits. Instead he raised his voice and chanted a third time:

"Brothers of the deep, O brothers of the deep!
Ho! for the coral strand.
Show yourselves near this land.
Break your blue sleep, shake your blue sleep!"

To the east and the west chanted the whale. To the north and the south he chanted. From the east and the west came his brothers, the tunas. From the north and the south they gathered, and after them came the bonitos and all manner of giant fishes until the waters of the Pacific were filled with the great whale's brothers.

The little sandpiper said nothing. He just sang again:

"Fair-feathers, fair-feathers,
Sail the spiced breeze.
Haste to these sandy-shored
Bright southern seas."

The sandpiper sang to the east and the west. To the north and the south he sang. From the east and the west came his brothers, the plovers. From the north and the south they flew down, and after them came the noddy terns and all manner of sea birds until the noise was like thunder and the sky black with wings.

And still no one knew whether there were more whales than sandpipers or more sandpipers than whales.

Then his brothers of the deep asked the great whale, "What shall we do now?"

"If we were to eat up all the land, the birds would die. Then even that stiff-necked sandpiper would have to admit that we outnumber his ranks," said the great whale.

"Very well," agreed his brothers and they began immediately to eat the land.

So then the birds asked the sandpiper, "What shall we do now?"

"If we were to drink up all the ocean, the fish would die. Then even that braggart whale would have to admit that we outnumber his brothers," said the little sandpiper.

"Very well," agreed the birds and they began immediately to drink up the ocean.

It took more time to eat the land than to drink the ocean. The birds were the first to finish. They had swallowed the ocean so fast that the cohorts of the great whale had had time to bite off only a little of the land.

But when the birds saw the fish gasping on the sea's sandy bottom, they had a second thought. With their larder dry, where, they began to wonder, would they find their food? For shore birds live off small fish and crabs and other creatures of the sea.

So first one bird then another coughed up the water he had swallowed so hastily. The ocean bed began to fill again and the fish revived and swam around as well as ever.

When all the water was back in the ocean, the brothers of the deep swam off to the south and the north and the west and the east and the great whale once more cut capers through the turquoise sea.

Then the birds flew off to the south and the north and the west and the east and the little sandpiper went back to running after crawfish in the reeds at the tide's edge.

To this day no one knows whether there are more whales in the world than sandpipers, or more sandpipers than whales.

The Firemakers

ONCE THERE WERE FOUR BROTHERS WHO WERE FISHERMEN. Maui, the eldest, liked to roam the flanks of that great peak, Mauna Kea.

At night in the chilly highlands, Maui often wished the gods of the volcano had shared with men the secret of fire. A man had to risk his life in the fumes and steam of its treacherous edge to get a coal from a crater. Maui longed to know how to kindle a fire.

One morning as the sun arrived in the east, Maui woke his brothers to go fishing. They launched their canoe and sped to the fishing grounds. Only a short time later Maui looked towards the shore and was surprised to see smoke rising near their harbor.

"Look," he said, "there is a fire! Whose can it be?"

"Whose indeed?" asked his brothers. "Let's get our fish and hurry back to see who has the secret. Perhaps today we can bake our catch."

So after they'd caught fish enough for dinner, they returned to shore. When the canoe neared the beach, Maui leaped out and ran to the place where he had seen the tell-tale smoke. He found nothing but ashes and some of his brothers' bananas, half-baked in the fire bed. Disappointed, he went back to the beach.

"Did you find a fire?" asked the others.

He shook his head, "Nothing there but ashes and half-baked bananas."

"Let's stay on shore," agreed the brothers, and for days they did not leave the island, hoping to come upon another fire. At last, tired of eating fruit and shore fish, they paddled again through the surf. No sooner had they reached the fishing grounds than smoke rose above the trees. A second time, they returned to find only a bed of ashes.

Then Maui said, "I will stay behind while you three go fishing. If I hide in the trees perhaps I can find out who makes the fires."

"Very well," answered his brothers, "we will fish for you while you get the fire for us," and they launched their canoe.

Though Maui stole up and down the shore, no fire appeared. He stayed behind many times but there was never a fire unless all the brothers had left the island. Then Maui thought of a way to fool the firemakers.

The next day he brought a huge calabash to the beach and dressed it in tapa so that from a distance it looked like Maui himself. Putting the calabash in the canoe, he tied it to his seat. When the fishermen splashed through the surf that day it looked as if all four of them had left the island. Maui hid in the trees and waited while his brothers took the dummy to the fishing grounds.

Soon he saw smoke rising near the beach. Silently, he made his way to the fire and discovered those possessive birds, the curly-tailed mudhens, roasting his brothers' bananas.

The fruit was not quite done when one of the mudhens sensed someone was watching and cried out, "Maui is a smart boy!"

Maui jumped from behind the trees. As the others flew off, he caught one old hen.

"You wretch," he thundered, "stealing our bananas and refusing to share your fire."

"Stop," croaked the mudhen, "if you choke me, the secret dies with me. If you let me live, I will show you how to make fire."

"Tell me where fire is and I'll let you live."

"In a green stick," lied the mudhen.

Maui rubbed together two green sticks. The sap ran down but no fire appeared.

"So, you would deceive me."

"Rub two reeds," quickly said the mudhen.

Maui rubbed them and they broke.

"You shall die," he warned the mudhen, twisting her neck.

Finally she showed him how to rub together dry chips and sandalwood. The fragrant smoke rose through the trees. Maui knew that at last he and his brothers could bake their fish and warm themselves on a cool night.

After scratching the top of her head until it was red to remind her of the way she had treated him, Maui let the mudhen go.

That is why, even now, the top of a mudhen's head is bare of feathers.

The Wiliwili Trees

ONCE THERE WERE FOUR SISTERS, MOHO-LANI, THE first-born, next Wiliwili-oheohe, then Wiliwili-peapea and last of all Wiliwili-kuapuu. Moho-lani was the most beautiful and her sisters were jealous of her, for Wiliwili-oheohe was bald and Wiliwili-peapea had a tangled mane of hair, while the shoulders of Wiliwili-kuapuu had grown round and ugly from laziness.

Now Moho-lani was the only sister who was married and she had one son named Kauila-makeha-okalani which means "Lightning-flashing-from-the-heavens." This son had been placed by Moho-lani and her husband under the protection of the gods and he lived with them in the land beyond the clouds.

Moho-lani's husband liked to walk along the shore watching the waves and the flying spray. He often went by a rocky point where two sea-witches sunned themselves. They admired his stalwart bearing, and one day by their mermaid chants lured him out to their rocks. With a kelp net they caught him and carried him to their deep sea cavern.

Weary with waiting for her husband's return, Moho-lani left her house to search for him. Finally on the beach she met two fishermen who had seen him disappear below the waves, snared fast in the sea-witches' net.

Then going to her sister, Moho-lani called:

"O Wiliwili-oheohe, come to my aid!
  O Wiliwili-oheohe, come to my aid!
Do you know if the mermaids have taken my husband
  To the place where the little stones rattle?"

But Wiliwili-oheohe, with her bald head, looked crossly at Moho-lani and answered, "Ugh, big, worthless man! I do not know where your husband is!"

Moho-lani walked on, weeping, to the second sister and called:

"O Wiliwili-peapea, come to my aid!
O Wiliwili-peapea, come to my aid!
Do you know if the mermaids have taken my husband
To the place where the little stones rattle?"

But Wiliwili-peapea, shaking her tangled hair, answered like her older sister, "Ugh, big, worthless man! I do not know where your husband is!"

Moho-lani went to her youngest sister and cried out the same words but she received the same answer, for Wiliwili-kuapuu, hunching her shoulders, said, "Ugh, big, worthless man! I do not know where your husband is!"

So no help came to Moho-lani from her jealous sisters.

Then she sought the gods who were her son's foster parents with the request that her son Kauila be allowed to leave them. And Kauila came to her aid.

In the ocean's cavern, he commanded the sea-witches to turn loose his father. Angry at their obstinacy, Kauila changed into a dart of lightning whose flame, zigzagging beneath the waves, slivered the sea-witches into a thousand pieces. (From them are sprung the fish called mackerel.) As soon as the sea-witches were transformed, Kauila's father was released.

Because of their unkindness to Moho-lani, the three sisters were changed into wiliwili trees. Since Wiliwili-oheohe was bald, she became an almost leafless tree; Wiliwili-peapea with her tangled hair turned into a tree whose leafy branches tossed in the wind; while lazy Wiliwili-kuapuu had a crooked trunk.

On the beach at Paula, the wiliwili trees are standing yet and the mackerel swim the ocean, for Kauila's parents had a son who could right wrongs.

PUERTO RICO

The Three-cornered Hat

PEDRO THE ROGUE LIVED BY HIS TRICKS. ALWAYS HE had been seen yesterday, or was expected tomorrow but no one could ever put a finger on him today.

One morning when Pedro's fortune had shrunk to a few hundred pesos, he stopped to consider this unhappy state of affairs. Then snatching his three-cornered hat, he set out for a store on the town square.

"Good day," said Pedro with great civility as he entered the shop.

"Good day, sir," bowed the proprietor.

"Would you do me a great favor?"

"At your service, sir."

"Have the goodness to keep a hundred pesos for me until I return with one corner of my hat folded over. Like so!"

To this unusual request the proprietor agreed.

Presently Pedro made his way to a store on the farther side of the square.

"Good day," said Pedro with great civility as he entered the shop.

"Good day, sir," bowed the proprietor.

"Would you do me a great favor?"

"At your service, sir."

"Have the goodness to keep a hundred pesos for me until I return with one corner of my hat folded over. Like so!"

To this unusual request the proprietor of the second store also agreed.

Immediately Pedro hastened to a store beyond the square. There too, the proprietor accepted a hundred pesos and promised to return the money when Pedro appeared with a corner of his hat folded over.

Hands in his pockets and hat on his head, Pedro walked gaily round the square. It was not long before he met a stranger to whom he gave a beguiling smile.

"Your spirits are very high," said the man.

"Who would not be happy with such a hat as I wear!" answered Pedro.

"And what is so remarkable about that hat?" asked the stranger.

"Come and see. It always brings me luck," invited

Pedro as he folded over one corner and set the hat back on his head.

Together they visited the three stores. In each one after a glance at the hat, the proprietor handed Pedro a hundred pesos.

"You see?" said Pedro to his companion as they left the third store. "Amazing, isn't it? This hat just whistles up the pesos when I need them."

"Wonderful," replied the stranger who had decided that he must have the marvelous hat.

"Perhaps you would sell it?" he asked.

"Perhaps," allowed Pedro.

"How much do you want for it?"

Pedro took off the hat and twirled it in his hand. "Oh," he said casually, "two thousand pesos."

"No, that's too much. I'll give you one thousand pesos," offered the stranger.

"Really, I should not sell it," answered Pedro, but handing the three-cornered hat to the stranger, he seized the thousand pesos and disappeared down a side street. The stranger did not see him again, for Pedro quickly put the town behind him.

Early the next morning the stranger set the hat on his head and went to the square. He wore it backwards, forwards and sideways, tilted and straight. He pushed in one, two and all three corners. But no one, in any of the dozen stores he visited, gave him so much as one peso.

Furious because the hat brought him no luck, he began to wonder and question and wonder again. At last it came to him that the wily wearer of the three-cornered hat had been none other than Pedro the Rogue. Taking the hat to the edge of town, he shot it full of holes. As its tattered corners sailed off in the wind, he cried out angrily:

"If you catch up with Pedro, shoot him for me!"

The Horse of Seven Colors

A KING THERE WAS, WHO HAD A BEAUTIFUL WHEAT field. The grain in the wind was a sight to make one glad but every dawn a mysterious creature trampled down another part of the field until half the wheat was gone.

The king called to his eldest son and said, "Spend the night in the field and capture the animal that is laying it waste."

So the eldest lad took a hammock to hang from a nearby tree and a guitar to keep him awake, and followed the setting sun to the clearing. As darkness spread over the field, he played song after song but by midnight sleep stilled his fingers and when morning broke, more wheat had been ruined.

The eldest son told his father what had happened and the angry king gave him a whipping. Then the second son bragged that he would capture the creature. He too took a hammock to hang from a tree and a guitar to keep him awake, but his success was no greater than that of his elder brother.

At last Juan Bobo, the youngest son, said to his father, "Papa, I will go tonight and see if I can catch the animal."

"You," said the king to Juan, "what are you thinking of? If your elder brothers couldn't catch it, why do you think you can? You are a *bobo*."

"Indeed so," agreed Juan, "but let me try."

The king, not bothering to answer, paid him no further attention. In the evening Juan, who had a mind of his own, made off with a hammock and a package of pins. He hung his hammock at the field's edge. Then, except for a place scarcely big enough to sit on, he stuck the pins, head up, all over it. Sitting there singing to himself, he waited out the night. Every time drowsiness pitched him over, the pins woke him up. Before cockcrow he heard the tread of an animal and was amazed to catch a magnificent horse whose coat boasted seven colors.

"If you will set me free," said the horse, "I will never return to the field, and to thank you I will give you seven hairs from my coat, each of a different color."

Juan accepted the seven hairs, freed the horse, and returned home. His brothers laughed his adventure to scorn but Juan showed the hairs to his father. From that day there was no further damage to the wheat.

A while later a neighboring king, a friend of Juan Bobo's father, decided it was high time his daughter should be married, but he wished to make sure his son-in-law would be a man of courage and ingenuity. The king called an assembly of his people and proclaimed that the man to bring him a perfect olive blossom would win his daughter.

Thereupon the princes from all around went off in search of the flower. Juan Bobo set out too but instead of taking a road, he followed a trail and lost himself at the foot of a mountain. Bewailing his luck he felt for the seven hairs in his pocket. Immediately the horse of seven colors was at his side.

"What's the trouble?" he asked.

"There's a neighboring king," answered Juan, "whose daughter is my love. Her father has promised her to the one who brings him a perfect olive blossom."

"Perfect olive flowers are hard come by," observed the horse, "but take heart and she shall be yours."

"How?" said Juan.

"You must journey to an enchanted castle. You will need a mount who knows the way. Climb on my back but first promise to give me my head."

"I promise," answered Juan and quickly mounted the horse whose coat boasted seven colors.

A fleet ride up the mountain brought them to a castle set on the rim of the clouds. The horse cantered into a deserted courtyard and stopped in front of a massive door. Juan slid off the horse's back.

"Enter," said the horse, "and do not hesitate to accept the hospitality of this place."

Juan pushed open the door. Going into a great hall, he saw a table set for dinner. There was not a sign of another human being, but remembering the horse's ad-

vice he quickly seated himself at the table. Many courses were served but to his amazement, he could see only the white hand which set the dishes before him. When he finished eating, a sweet voice spoke, "Come, let us go to the garden."

Juan followed the voice into a high-walled patio and watched the white hand pick a blossom.

"Here is a perfect olive flower," said the voice. "I will place it inside this flask. When the moment comes to present it, say, 'Hail, white hand!' and remove the silver stopper."

Juan took the flask, bowed his thanks to the voice's invisible owner and found the horse of seven colors waiting for him in the courtyard. He mounted and again gave the horse his head. Quickly they made their way down the mountain.

People were gathering to witness the contest when Juan arrived at the neighboring king's. On the edge of the throng, the horse halted.

"It is time for us to part," he said, and as soon as Juan put foot to the ground, the horse disappeared in the direction of the mountain.

Carrying his precious flask, Juan hastened to where the group of young princes waited impatiently, each with a flower in hand. They hailed him with cries of, "Here comes the *bobo* without a blossom."

When the judging hour came the contestants, one by one, presented their flowers to the king. Beautiful as they were, not one was a perfect olive blossom. On each some tiny blemish marred the stem or petals.

The last in turn was Juan Bobo. Standing before the king he said in a low voice, "Hail, white hand!" and opened the flask. An exquisite blossom burst forth. It was an olive flower of absolute perfection.

Overcome by its beauty, the king was slow to speak. At last he said, "My people, here is the winner."

Immediately, the crowd acclaimed Juan the chosen bridegroom. He married the princess and theirs was a merry match with many a ride on the horse whose coat boasted seven colors.

The Fig Tree

THERE WAS ONCE AN OLD WOMAN WHO HAD A GOAT. One day some men passed by carrying fig switches. They dropped one and the old woman planted it in her garden thinking the while what a fine fig tree time would bring. But the goat, when the fig switch took root and began to put out tender shoots, ate up branches and all. Into the garden went the old woman as the goat was chewing the last tender shoot.

"Goat," she exclaimed, "give me my fig tree. This fig tree was not mine. It was the men's who passed by the road."

Then the goat lost one of its horns. The old woman picked it up and went to the river to wash it. The river swept it out of her hands. Then she exclaimed:

"River, give me my horn. This horn was not mine. It was the goat's. The goat ate my fig tree. The fig tree was not mine. It was the men's who passed by the road."

Then the river gave her a fish. She went to the house to broil it but the fire scorched the fish. Then the old woman exclaimed:

"Fire, give me my fish. This fish was not mine. It was the river's. The river took my horn. The horn was not mine. It was the goat's. The goat ate my fig tree. The fig tree was not mine. It was the men's who passed by the road."

The fire gave her an ax, but along came a woodcutter

who borrowed the ax on condition that the first sticks of wood should belong to the old woman. But the woodcutter broke the ax. Then the old woman exclaimed:

"Woodcutter, give me my ax. The ax was not mine. It was the fire's. The fire scorched my fish. The fish was not mine. It was the river's. The river took my horn. The horn was not mine. It was the goat's. The goat ate my fig tree. The fig tree was not mine. It was the men's who passed by the road."

Then the woodcutter gave her a piece of wood. Along came an ironing woman who borrowed the piece of wood promising to the old woman the first skirt she ironed. But the piece of wood turned to ashes and the old woman exclaimed:

"Ironing woman, give me my piece of wood. It was not mine. It was the woodcutter's. The woodcutter broke my ax. The ax was not mine. It was the fire's. The fire scorched my fish. The fish was not mine. It was the river's. The river took my horn. The horn was not mine. It was the goat's. The goat ate my fig tree. The fig tree was not mine. It was the men's who passed by the road."

Then the ironing woman gave her a skirt, and the old woman was so delighted that she didn't say another word.

VIRGIN ISLANDS

Ol' Guinea Man

THERE WAS ONCE A KING WHOSE WIFE ALWAYS HAD the last word. Tired of her carping tongue, the king declared that any man who could call his wife a liar would be rewarded with a portion of his riches.

Ol' Guinea man, passing by, heard of the offered prize. Eager to share the king's wealth, he stepped right in and said, "Good evening, lady!"

"Good evening, gentleman!"

"Can you tell me how many months in a year?"

"Yes," she said.

"Well," said Ol' Guinea man, "I don't know, an' I would like to know de different names of de months."

"Well, I am going to teach you dem; you will say after me."

Then she started.

She said, "January."

He said, "January."

She said, "February," and he said, "February."
She said, "March," and he said, "March."
She said, "April."
He said, "April."
She said, "May," and he said, "May."
She said, "June," and he said, "June."
She said, "July," and he said, "*You lie.*"
She said, "You can't talk better dan dat?"
"No."

Well, it went to contest and Ol' Guinea man, because he could not speak better, won the king's riches.

Crafty Crab

"YOU ALL THE TIME BUSY, MR. FOX?" ASKED BROTHER Crab.

Brother Fox made no answer.

"Why you not walk slow like me? You can run very fast but I'll run you a race. Let us bet," said Brother Crab, "that I win."

"How much will you bet me?" asked Brother Fox.

"I'll bet you two cents to every mile that I get in first."

They took their places by the starting pole.

Then Brother Crab said, "Mr. Fox, we ready now to go, but turn your tail. Let me see how safe your tail be. You can't run faster than me. I will give you one head in front."

As Brother Fox turned himself around so that Brother Crab could inspect his tail, the crab took a firm hold on his thick brush. It was in fine shape and Brother Crab held fast to it.

"All right. Let us go," called out Brother Fox. Without so much as a look around, he was off in a cloud of sand, the crab riding his tail as it sailed through the air behind him.

When Brother Fox reached the winning pole, he turned around to see how far behind he had left Brother Crab. His tail touched the pole and his challenger dropped to the ground beside it.

Brother Fox looked this way and that trying to spot the crab back somewhere in the sand. Then came a voice from the winning pole.

"What are you looking for? I am here long, waiting on you."

And that was the way the crab won the race.

The Sailor and the Devil's Daughter

WELL, THERE WAS A SAILOR, A YOUNG FELLOW, NAMED Jack. At sea, Jack and the captain once got into such an argument that the captain gave him a loaf of bread and threw him overboard.

With the bread on his head, Jack swam and swam until he reached Devil's Island. There on the beach he met an old woman, and that old woman was the devil's mother.

"Say, Jack, give us a piece of your bread!" said she.

He gave her a piece of the bread and she asked him, "What are you doing here?"

"I'm looking for work," answered Jack.

"Go to yonder river where my three granddaughters are bathing," she advised. "Take the youngest one's clothes and hide them. It's she who knows all the devil's secrets. Then wait until you hear her call, 'Whoever will find my clothes, I'll do anything in my power for him!' "

Jack went to the edge of the river, hid the youngest girl's clothes, and climbed up a tree to wait. When the swimming party was over, the girls began to dress. The youngest searched and searched but could not find her clothes. So her impatient sisters left her behind ransacking the bushes.

Finally the youngest girl called out, "Whoever will find my clothes, I'll do anything in my power for him."

At these words, Jack came down from the tree and found the clothes for her, and she said, "Now, what do you want for your kindness?"

"Work," said Jack.

"Come to my father, please," she answered, "but let me see him first. Then you tell him you want work."

So Jack did just that.

"Well," said the devil, "I have some things I want done. If you can do them, as much gold as you can carry will be yours; if you fail, you become one of my imps."

The following day the first task the devil set was cleaning a seven-horse stable which hadn't been swept for six years. Jack was to make it so clean that the devil could see his face in the floor.

With a shovel, pickax, and rake Jack went to work. The harder he tried to clean the stable, the dirtier it became. So at twelve o'clock, just where he'd started was as far as he'd gone.

Then said the devil, for his wife had readied dinner, "Who will carry Jack food?"

"I wouldn't be seen carrying a sailor's food," answered his youngest daughter.

For being so impudent, the devil told her she would be the one to take the food to Jack. That was just what she wanted. So she went to Jack and found him asleep. Waking him, she said, "Don't be alarmed! I will clean those stables for you."

She took seven cows and threw one in each stall and

in five minutes' time everything was clean enough for the devil to see his face in the floor. Then Jack went back to sleep.

Five o'clock and the devil came. To his surprise, he saw the work was done. However, he had other tasks up his sleeve, so he said, "Well, Jack, you've done fine but tomorrow brings another day."

In the morning the devil took Jack to a bottomless river. There he pounded a big diamond ring as fine as dust and threw it into the water.

"Dive in the river and bring up the diamond whole again," ordered the devil and he left Jack alone.

At twelve o'clock his wife readied dinner and the devil called out, "Who will carry Jack food?"

"I wouldn't be seen carrying a sailor's food. I took it yesterday; I'll not take it today," said the youngest daughter.

The devil told her for being so impudent again she would be the one to take the food to Jack. So she carried the food and a big empty dish as well.

"Jack," she said, "first throw me into the dish, then toss the dish into the river."

He hurled them into the river. When she came up, she brought the ring with her and gave it back to Jack.

"By midnight," she warned him, "my father will be after us."

When five o'clock and the devil came, he saw that Jack had the ring and the diamond was whole. The devil began to suspect his youngest daughter—she was the only one who knew his secrets.

Now the devil had two horses. One could leap a thousand miles and the other ten times a thousand. He also had an old rooster who used to tell him everything that went on.

That night Jack put the heart of a banana tree in his bed. When the devil came at midnight, he struck the banana heart with a sledge hammer and laughed to think he had rid himself of Jack. Then he went back to sleep, but before daybreak his old rooster started to crow:

"The two young rebels done gone!"

So the devil up and listened. The rooster crowed again:

"The two young rebels done gone!"

The devil went to his youngest daughter's room and found her bed empty. Then the rooster sang out a third time:

"The two young rebels done gone!"

Going to the stable, the devil found only one horse. He jumped on it and said, "Leap, Nick, ten thousand miles."

Three times he said it.

Now Jack and the youngest daughter were ahead on

the horse that leaped thousand-mile leaps. When the girl looked behind and saw her father coming, she dropped a kernel of corn.

Immediately, the horse became a pond, the girl a duck, and Jack a fisherman sitting on the bank with his pole.

The devil rode up to the duck and asked, "Have you seen my daughter and Jack here?"

The duck answered, "The water's very nice. Will you come and have a bath?"

"I didn't ask you that," said the devil. "I asked if you'd seen my daughter and Jack?"

The duck dove beneath the water so the devil went home and told his wife.

"The duck was your daughter, the pond her horse,

and that man fishing was Jack. Go and get them," said she.

The devil rode out again. His youngest daughter saw him coming and dropped another kernel. The horse became a churchyard, the girl an old lady on her way to prayers, and Jack a priest.

The devil said to the priest, "Have you seen a man and my daughter pass here on a horse?"

The priest asked the devil, "Would you like to light a candle?"

The devil said again, "Have you seen a man and my daughter pass here on a horse?"

"Would you like to be saved?" asked the priest.

The devil jumped over the wall and went home to his wife.

"The churchyard was the horse, the old lady on her way to prayers your daughter, and the priest was Jack," said she. "Go and get them."

With a leap the devil returned. His youngest daughter saw him coming and threw out her last kernel. Between the girl and the devil came up a great river, too wide to jump. So the devil's horse started to drink it dry but there was so much water that the devil, in his hurry, began to drink too.

Then the devil's horse burst and the devil burst, but Jack and the youngest daughter were married at a big party with a big cake.

An' the wheel bend,
An' the story end.

About the Stories in This Book

The collection of American folktales, *With a Wig, With a Wag*, contained only stories from the mainland. There are many Americans living on Pacific and Caribbean islands as well as in Alaska. Their tales add greatly to the American heritage.

Alaska is a treasure house of Eskimo legends. The stories of Hawaii are Polynesian in origin. Spain and Africa have contributed to the lore of Puerto Rico while the American Virgin Islands were for many years in contact with Danish customs. If we do not know these tales from beyond the mainland as well as our familiar Indian, European, and Negro stories, we miss a rich variety of beauty, humor, and folk tradition.

The Stories from Alaska

There are many tales among the original Americans, the Indians, concerning the sun, moon, and stars, for they were a people who lived close to nature. Going north along the Pacific coast, legends of the sun become increasingly important as the hours of light grow fewer and more precious.

Raven figured in many stories of the northwest. In "The Extraordinary Black Coat" from the Yukon valley it is he who brings back the sun in a story which also accounts for the origin of ravens. The shamans were the medicine men who conducted the ceremonies of the tribe. This version is based on "The Bringing of the Light by Raven" in *The Eskimo About Bering Strait* by Edward William Nelson, in Part I of the 18th Annual Report of the Bureau of American Ethnology, 1896-97, Washington, D.C., Government Printing Office, 1899.

There are several kinds of bears in Alaska but the grizzlies are the fiercest. The myth on which "The Cranberry Feast" is based was recorded in English at Wrangell early in 1904. It was related by an old man named Kasank. It is curious that cranberries which we associate with our Thanksgiving and Christmas dinners, should have been served at this feast of fellowship between the grizzlies and the old hunter.

The path of light in "Whistle the Winds" is the galaxy which appears in many Eskimo stories as well as in tales all over the world. In China it is spoken of as a river, in Europe a highway. To the man looking for the tree on the tundra, as the Arctic plains are called, it also seemed to be a road. We often call it the Milky Way. If you go out in the evening, especially when the moon is dark, you can see this great star-studded band circling the sky. Our tale is retold from "The Origin of Winds" in *The Eskimo About Bering Strait* by Edward William Nelson as mentioned above.

"Whale of a Tale" is a story of the Seward peninsula gathered by the curator-librarian of the Alaskan Historical Museum and Library. An igloo is a house made of ice blocks. Blubber is whale fat and an oogrook is a large bearded seal.

Most Eskimo tales were told by men in their meeting-houses, but the story, "Dance, Raven, Dance," from Norton Bay is a woman's tale especially meant for children to enjoy. It is a retelling of "The Raven and the Marmot," also found in Edward William Nelson's *The Eskimo About Bering Strait.*

The Stories from Hawaii

The islands of Hawaii are on the northern edge of the Polynesian cultural area of the south Pacific Ocean. There are many stories in this region, basically alike but varying in detail with local tradition.

One of the best guides to Hawaiian pronunciation appears in *The Picture Story of Hawaii* by Hester O'Neill (David McKay Company, Inc., 1950). The author says, "The music and the language of Hawaii are both soft and sliding. The language can almost be called a form of music, and it will be very easy for you to pronounce Hawaiian words if you remember a few simple things. The language is made up mostly of the five vowels. There are only twelve letters in the alphabet, the five vowels and seven consonants, H, K, L, M, N, P, and W. If W comes in the middle of a word, it is pronounced as if it were V. At the beginning of the word it is just like the English W. Every vowel is a separate syllable." Therefore, Oahu is o-AH-hoo, Maui is Mah-oo-ee, and ohia is o-HEE-ah.

Pikoi was a legendary hero of Hawaii. Especially in the islands' feudal period, heroes frequently proved themselves in contests. A bowl-shaped container is called a calabash. Since Hawaiians knew nothing of the potter's art, these were most often made of coconut shells, gourds or carved from a hard wood. They were used for many purposes. Before metal was imported to make mirrors, pools of water were used as reflectors and tricks performed with them. So it is not surprising in "The Magic Calabash" to have a water-filled calabash used as a mirror. The ohia is the monkey pod tree. Its wood is used for trays, calabashes, and other articles.

Guessing riddles was a popular type of Hawaiian contest. Papa and Wakea, legendary ancestors of the Hawaiians, supposedly lived near the present site of Honolulu. "The Queen's Riddles" is a retelling of "The Chief with the Wonderful Servants" in *Legends of Old Honolulu* by W. D. Westervelt; Boston, Geo. H. Ellis Co., 1915. This tale was first published in a native newspaper in 1862. All who know the Grimms' "Six Servants," will recognize the theme of the peculiarly gifted servants aiding their master.

From the Marshall Islands southeast of Hawaii comes the story "Coral Sea Contest." This favorite bedtime chant can go on and on by naming more birds and fish as allies of the sandpiper and whale. It is one of many legends indigenous to Micronesia which were gathered into readers by the United States Navy. There were so many dialects in the various islands that the natives could hardly understand each other, much less the Americans. It was hoped that the Micronesian readers, made up of stories familiar to all the children, would further a common language among them.

There are tales similar to "The Firemakers" in the lore of all primitive peoples. Our story is based on "The Origin of Fire," in *Hawaiian Folk Tales*, compiled by Thomas G. Thrum; Chicago, A. C. McClurg & Co., 1907. In Hawaii, the legendary hero Maui is considered to be the one who learned how to kindle fire. Tapa, beat out from the bark of the paper mulberry into a soft fabric, is the native cloth of the islands.

"The Wiliwili Trees" is one of a group of pure Hawaiian folk tales from the Kau district on the island of Hawaii. The wiliwili is actually a homely, crooked tree that has either many or few leaves. Because of the buoyancy of its wood, it was often used to carve the outriggers on the canoes called by that name.

The Stories from Puerto Rico

Most Puerto Rican tales are Spanish in origin. There are cycles of stories about both Pedro the Mischief-Maker and Juan Bobo, the seemingly foolish youth who wins out by his ingenuity. Both these characters have their counterparts in Spain but they have made Puerto Rico their home. The peso mentioned in "The Three-cornered Hat" is a silver coin.

"The Fig Tree" reminds us of accumulative tales around the world. Perhaps the best known of this type is "The House that Jack Built" in *Mother Goose.*

The Stories from the Virgin Islands

"Ol' Guinea Man" uses the device of making one person say another has lied and thereby winning a prize. This story from St. Croix island is a little like "The Ashlad Who Made the Princess Say 'You Lie' " in Sigrid Undset's *True and Untrue and Other Norse Tales.*

A race between a fast animal and a slow one who wins by his wits is another world-wide theme. Our story of the crafty crab is also from St. Croix. No doubt the classic example is the English "The Hare and the Hedgehog" in Walter de la Mare's *Told Again.*

There are many Jack tales in England and in the Southern Highlands of the United States. In "The Sailor and the Devil's Daughter," Jack has turned sailor like so many of the Danes to whom the island of St. Thomas, the home of this tale, once belonged. The tag rhyme is an ending often used in stories from the Virgin islands.

THE MAGIC CALABASH:

Folk Tales from America's Islands and Alaska

Edited by Jean Cothran

ILLUSTRATED BY CLIFFORD N. GEARY

The Magic Calabash takes up where *With a Wig, With a Wag* left off. The latter contained American folk tales only from the mainland; the new book completes the collection with a fine group from areas now also American: Alaska, Hawaii, Puerto Rico, and the Virgin Islands. The folk lore of these regions adds greatly to the American heritage because it too comes from widely diverse cultures.

Like folk tales the world over, some of the stories stem from a common past. For instance, it is interesting to find in "The Queen's Riddles," a tale from Hawaii, echoes of "The Six Servants" by the Brothers Grimm. Universal folk themes crop up here as they do elsewhere. The well-known race between a fast animal and a slow one is the theme of the delightful "Crafty Crab" from St. Croix; while the ever-popular accumulative tale, best known perhaps in "The House That Jack Built," turns up in a charming bit, "The Fig Tree," from Puerto Rico.

But many of the stories are completely indigenous. In these lands, too, early peoples wondered about the sun and the moon and the winds; the miracles of day and night and the changing seasons; the astonishing variety of trees and flowers and birds and fish; the strange phenomenon called man. Their thoughts and their deeds involving all this have come down to us in legends